DISNEY'S

LION

MUFASA's LITTLE
INSTRUCTION BOOK

DISNEY
PRESS

Library of Congress Catalog Card Number: 94-70989
ISBN: 0-7868-4015-3

3   5   7   9   10   8   6   4   2

Every night when darkness begins to fall on the Pride Lands, my dad—King Mufasa—and I sit beneath the stars. And as we are looking up at the sky, he tells me all sorts of things, things that make me laugh and things that make me wonder. Sometimes he tells me about what it takes to become a great lion and a respected king. Here are some of the wise words he's shared with me. My dad says if I can remember what he's told me, I'll have no trouble following in his paw prints.

Simba

☀ Pounce at every challenge.

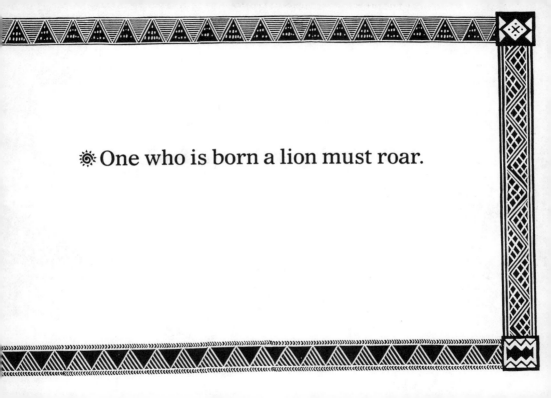

One who is born a lion must roar.

☀ Don't play with your food.

☀ Always lick your paws
after you have eaten.

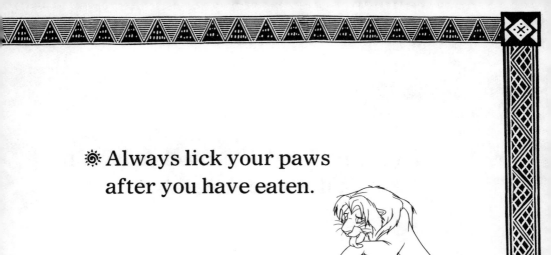

☀ Very little in life is black and white—
except if you're a zebra!

☀ Always think before you roar.

❀ Don't choose your friends based on the color of their fur, where they live, or their species.

☀ "No act of kindness, no matter how
small, is ever wasted."

—*Aesop*

☀ Be brave only when you have to be—
don't go looking for trouble.

☀ Never ride an ostrich
on a full stomach.

☀ A father's footsteps
are large and deep.

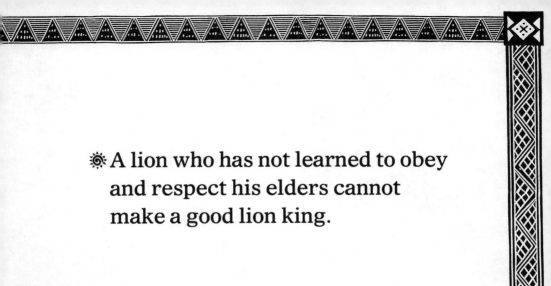

☀ A lion who has not learned to obey and respect his elders cannot make a good lion king.

☀ Don't be sneaky with Rafiki.

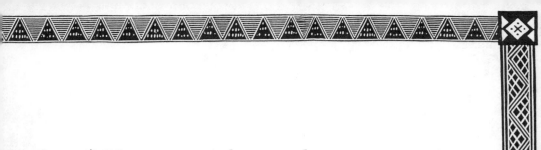

☀ If you try to be too sharp,
   you'll cut yourself.

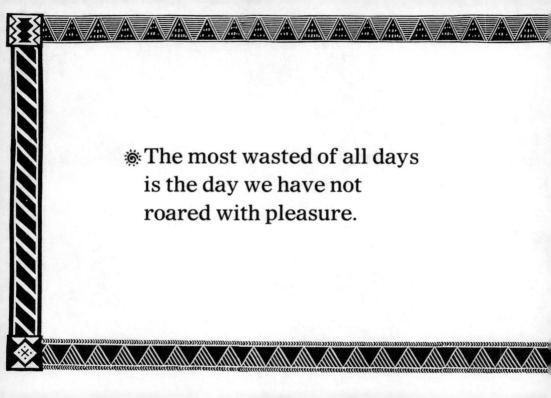

❋ The most wasted of all days
is the day we have not
roared with pleasure.

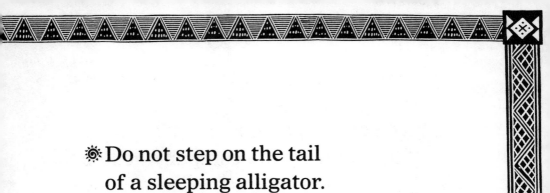

☀ Do not step on the tail
of a sleeping alligator.

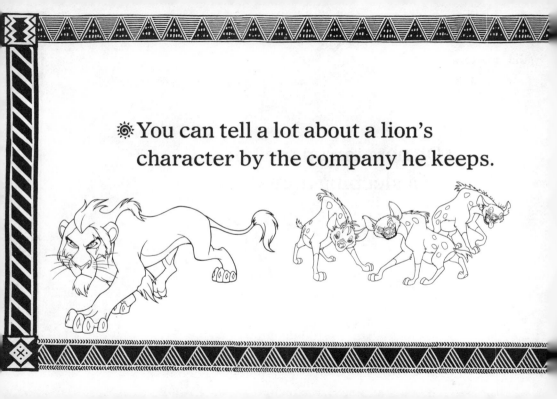

☀ You can tell a lot about a lion's character by the company he keeps.

☀ Some animals are wise,
and some are otherwise.
—*inspired by Tobias Smollett*

☀ Never blow your nose
in an elephant's ear.

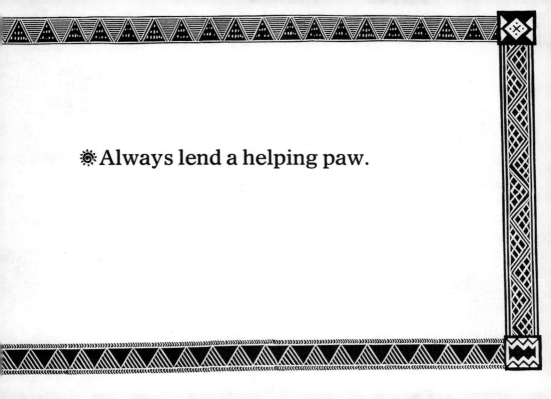

☀ Always lend a helping paw.

☀ Where hyenas wrangle,
drool will dangle.

☀ Good taste is in the
mouth of the beholder.

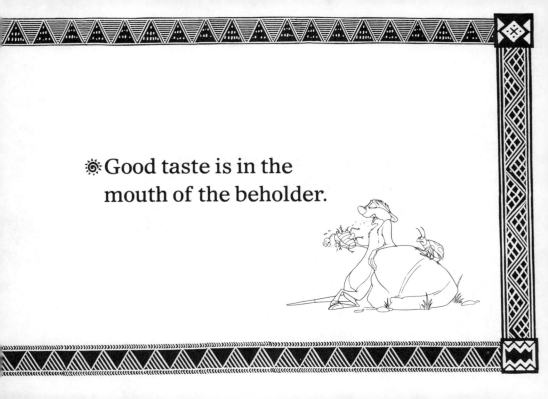

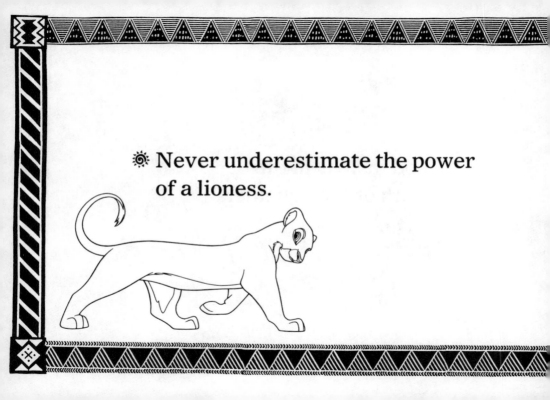

☀ Never underestimate the power of a lioness.

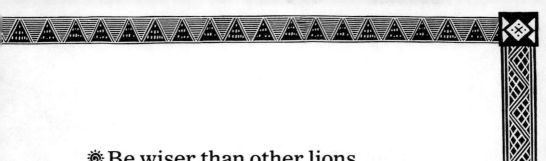

☀ Be wiser than other lions,
but do not tell them so.

☀ Only the antelope can jump
to conclusions.

☀ A compromise is the art of
dividing a zebra in such a way
that everyone believes he or she
has the biggest piece.

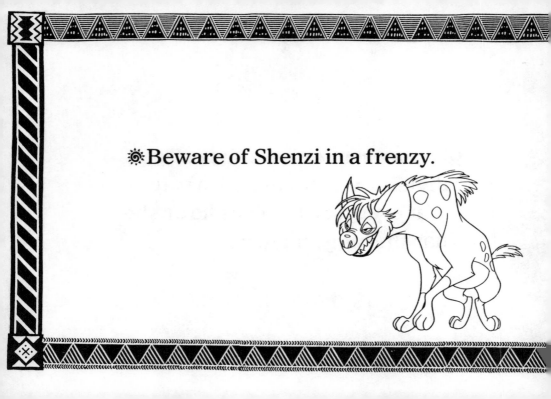

☀ Beware of Shenzi in a frenzy.

☀ A lion who does not remember his mistakes will repeat them.

☀ Understand the balance of nature
and respect all the creatures—
from the crawling ant to
the leaping antelope.

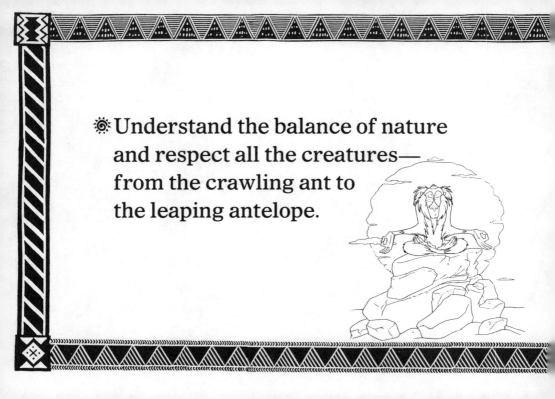

☀ "There is enough for the needy,
but not enough for the greedy."
—*M. K. Gandhi*

☀ When a lion is wrapped up in himself,
he makes a pretty small package.

☀ No lion is an island, entire of itself;
every lion is part of a pride.
—*inspired by John Donne*

☀ If you're thirsty,
follow the water buffalo.

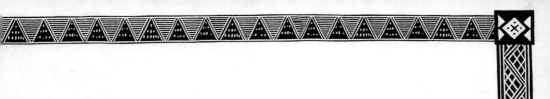

☀ Home is where your rump rests.

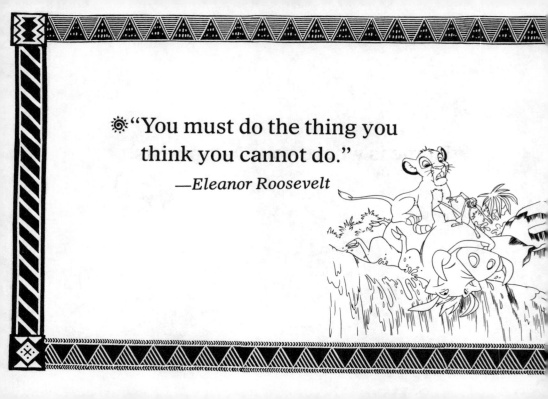

☀ "You must do the thing you think you cannot do."

—*Eleanor Roosevelt*

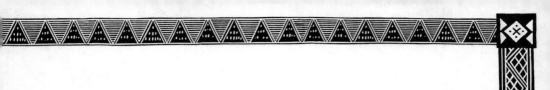

☀ Every lion king should learn to do one thing very well because he likes it and one thing very well because he doesn't like it.

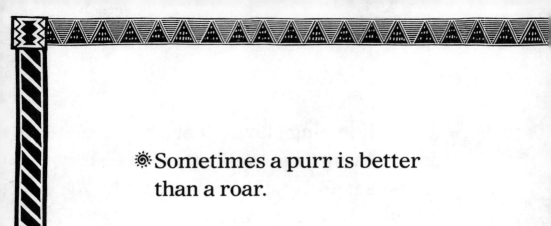

☀ Sometimes a purr is better than a roar.

☀ "When all think alike,
 then no one is thinking."
 —*Walter Lippmann*

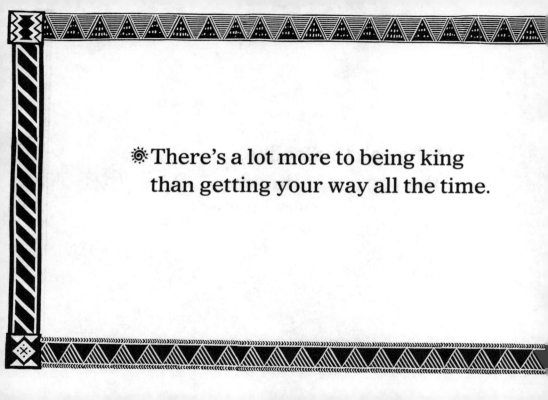

✦ There's a lot more to being king
than getting your way all the time.

☀ If you cannot catch your dinner,
do not blame the savannah.

☼ You can always tell a hornbill,
but you can't tell him much.

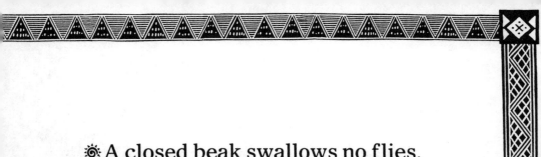 A closed beak swallows no flies.

☀ Earth and stone make a lion's den,
but happy lion cubs make a home.

☀ Smile and the world smiles with you—
unless you're a hyena.

☀ The only way to have a friend
is to be one.

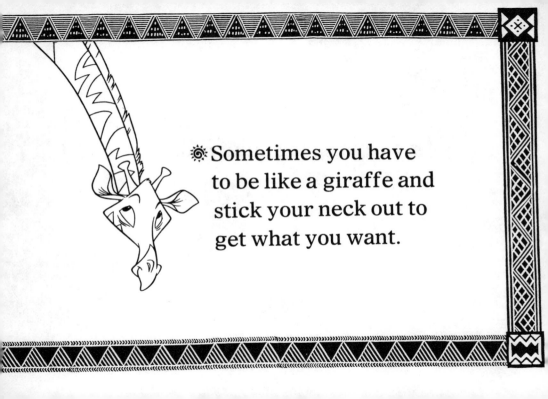

Sometimes you have to be like a giraffe and stick your neck out to get what you want.

☀ Leave no log unturned.

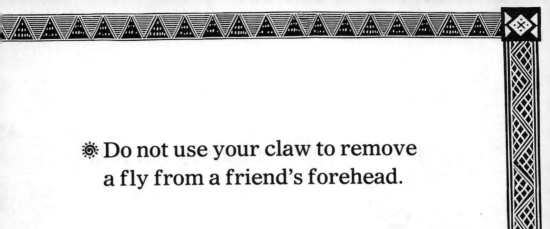

☀ Do not use your claw to remove
a fly from a friend's forehead.

❖ Always put your best paw forward.

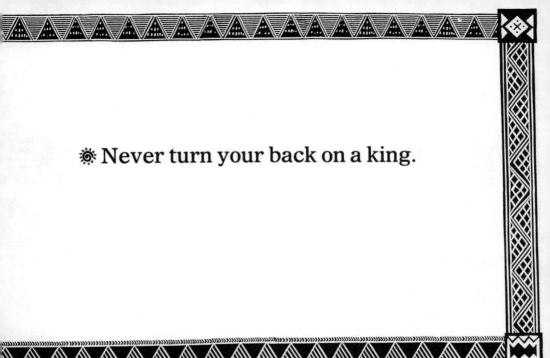

☀ Never turn your back on a king.

☀ If you do not save the land around you, it will not save you.

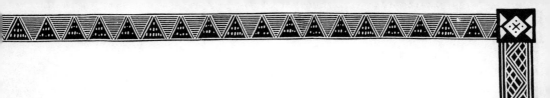

☀ Don't accept a dinner invitation
from a hyena. He may just be serving
whatever's "lion" around!

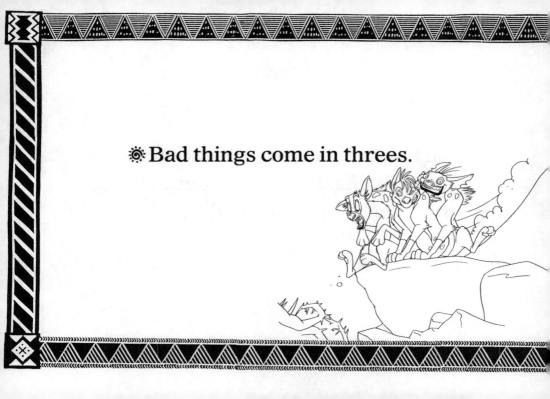

☀ Bad things come in threes.

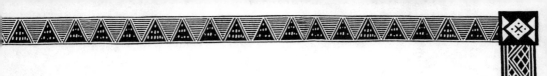

☀️There are those animals who laugh
to show their sharp teeth, and
there are those animals who cry
to show their good hearts.

☀ Weak lions are apt to be cruel.

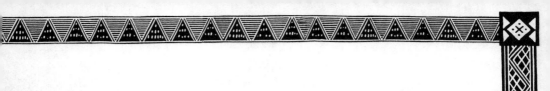

☀ You can accomplish by kindness
what you cannot do by force.

☀ When elephants fight, it is the grass that suffers.

☀️He who laughs last is Ed.

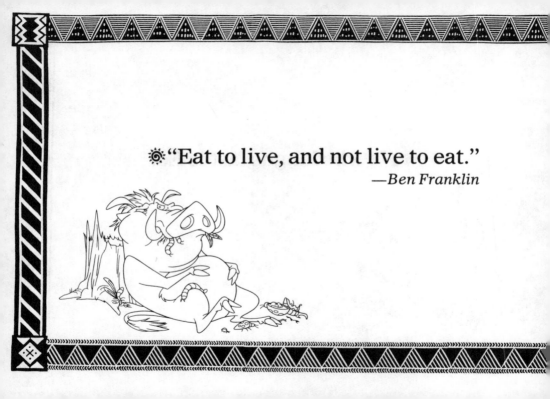

☼ "Eat to live, and not live to eat."
—*Ben Franklin*

☀A barren savannah is a poor hunting ground.

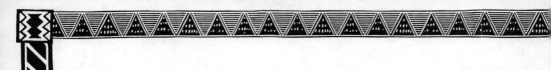

☀ "Injustice anywhere is a threat
to justice everywhere."

—*Martin Luther King, Jr.*

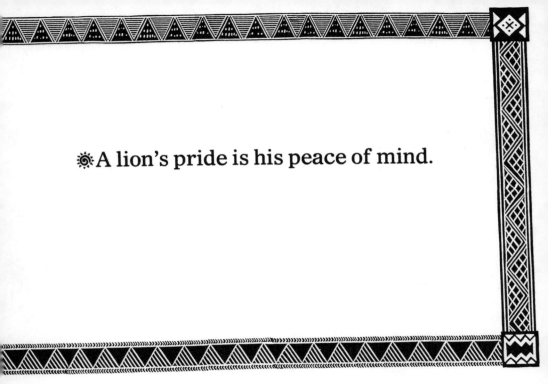

☀A lion's pride is his peace of mind.

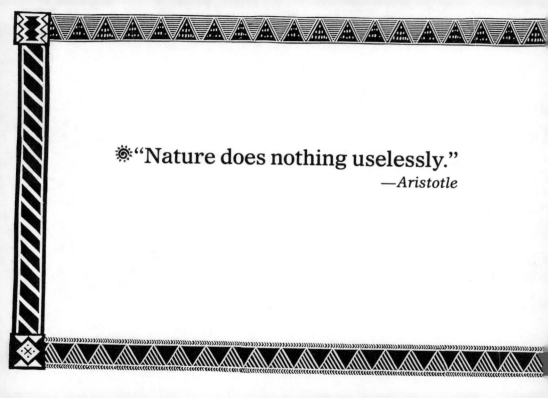

☀ "Nature does nothing uselessly."
　　　　　　　　　　　　　—*Aristotle*

☀A bathing warthog gathers no mud.

☀ All smiles are not equal.

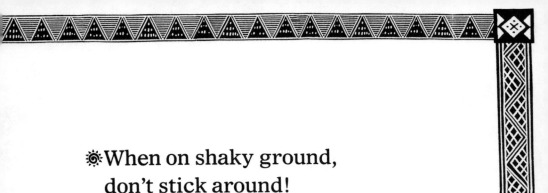

☀When on shaky ground,
don't stick around!

※A hungry lion is not a free lion.

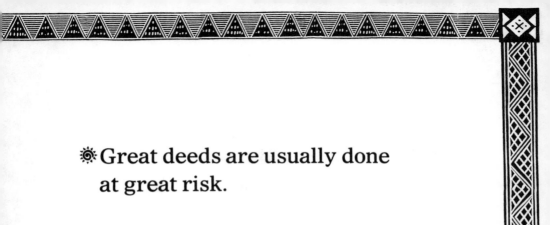

☀ Great deeds are usually done
at great risk.

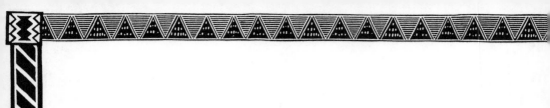

☀ Trust your elders—
your life is in their hands.

☀ Many paws make light work.

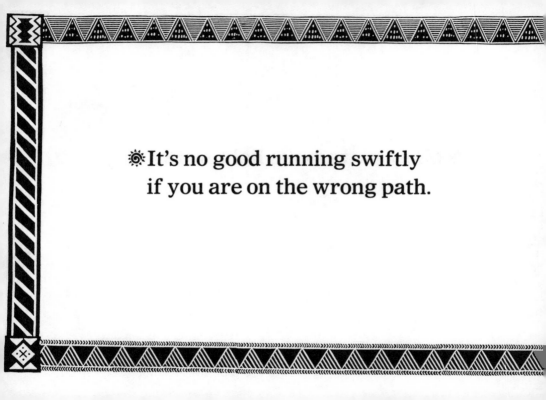

☀ It's no good running swiftly
if you are on the wrong path.

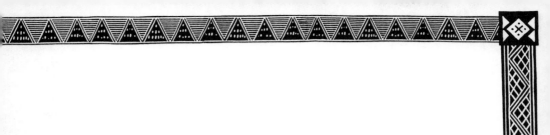

☀ To speak without thinking
is to pounce without first
seeing your prey.

A lion king must not judge
until he has heard both sides
of the argument.

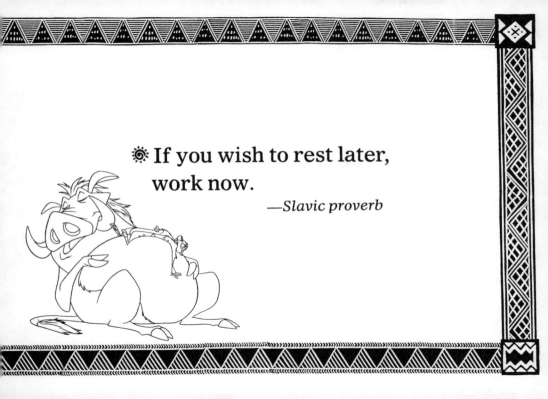

☀ If you wish to rest later,
work now.

—*Slavic proverb*

☀Wisdom is the sunlight of the soul.

☀ No lion ever became great
by being a copycat.

☀ Only a foolish lion thinks he knows everything.

☀ It's good to clear the air
among friends—especially
if you're a warthog!

☀ To climb the mountain,
  you must begin at the bottom.

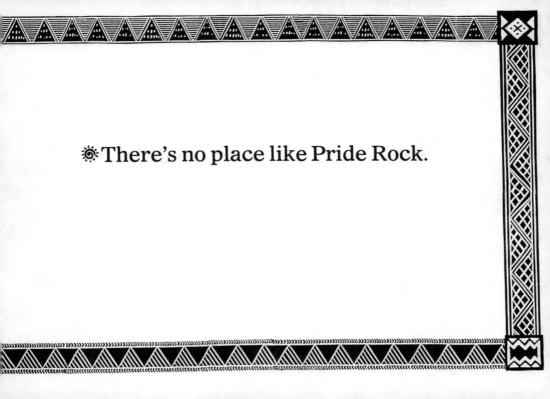

☀There's no place like Pride Rock.

☀ There is no such thing as a mere cat, only meerkats.

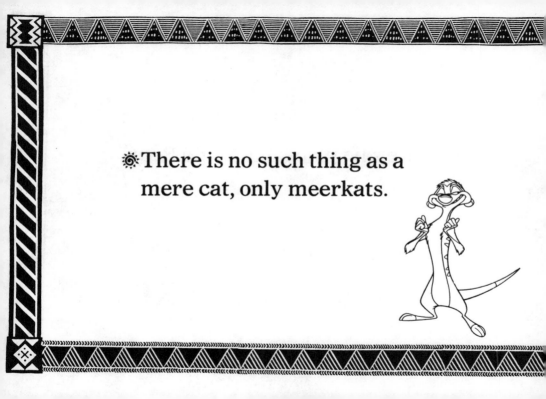

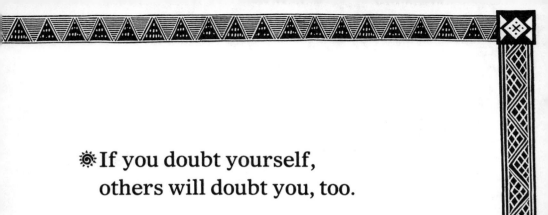

☀ If you doubt yourself,
  others will doubt you, too.

☀Don't bite the paw that feeds you.

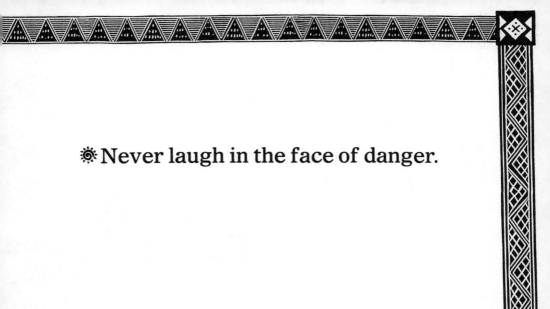

☀ Never laugh in the face of danger.

☀There's wisdom in the tune
of the old baboon.

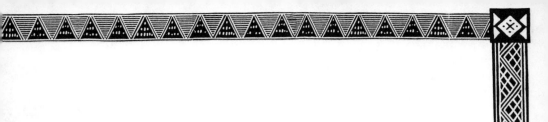

☀All wise animals know that the purpose of life is to enjoy it.

☀Do not lie beneath the buzzards.

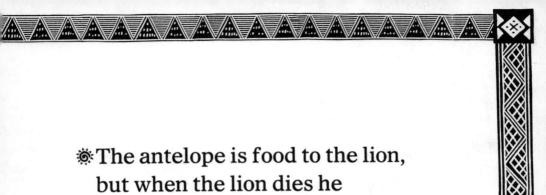

The antelope is food to the lion, but when the lion dies he becomes the grass and so feeds the antelope.

☀ A lion learns to pounce only by trying again and again.

☀ "Be a good animal, true to your animal instincts."

—*D. H. Lawrence*

☀ You may have to fight a battle
more than once to win it.

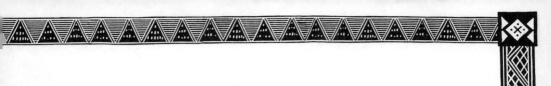

☀If your roar is small, do not expect
to catch large prey.

☀ You've got to put your behind
in the past.

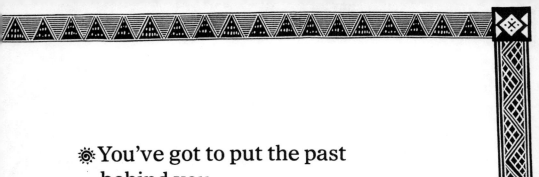

☀ You've got to put the past behind you.

☀ Always stand upwind
from a warthog.

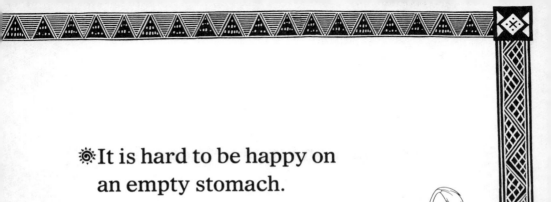

☀ It is hard to be happy on an empty stomach.

☀ Even lion kings get scared.

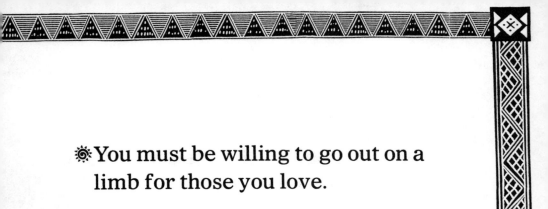

※ You must be willing to go out on a limb for those you love.

☀Don't underestimate a meerkat in a hula skirt.

☀Share your courage with others.

☀ "Speak softly and carry a big stick."

—*Teddy Roosevelt*

☀ No lion can think clearly when his paws are clenched.

☀ Change is good, but it's not easy.

☀ Your eyes are of little use if
your mind is closed.
                    —*Arab proverb*

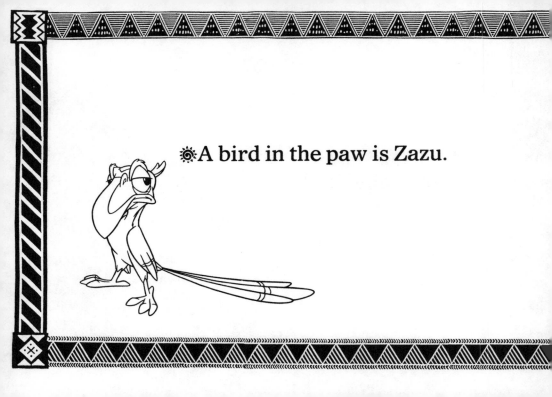

☀A bird in the paw is Zazu.

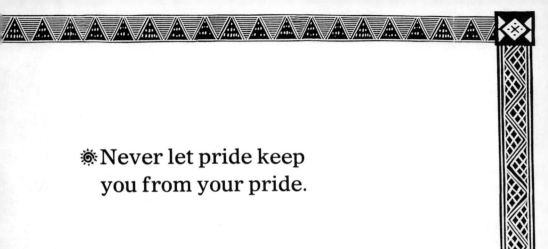
❂ Never let pride keep
you from your pride.

☀ True love doesn't fade,
it deepens.

☀ A faint heart never
wins a fair lioness.

☀ A lyin' lion is no better
than a cheetah.

☀A clear conscience makes
a sound sleep.

—Scottish proverb

☀ The question is, Who are you?

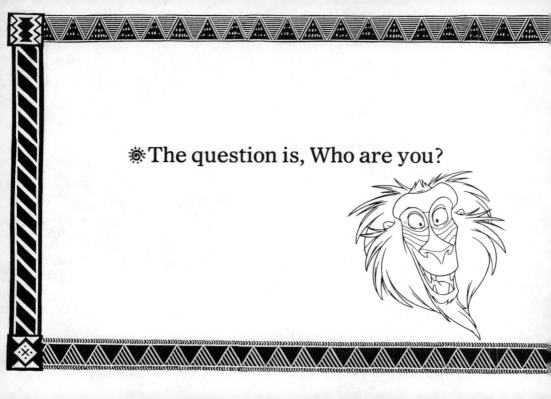

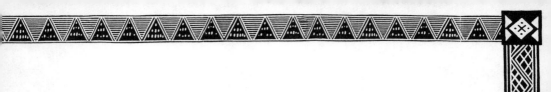

❂Nothing can bring you
peace but yourself.

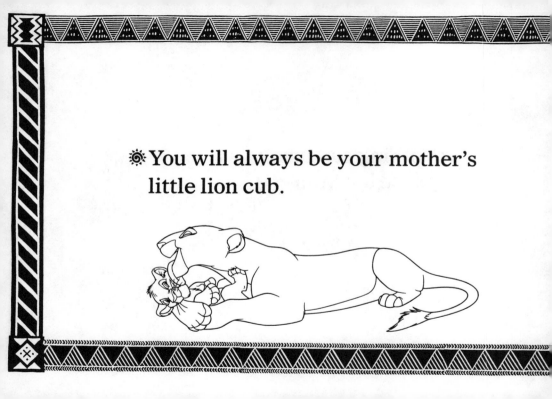

❀ You will always be your mother's little lion cub.

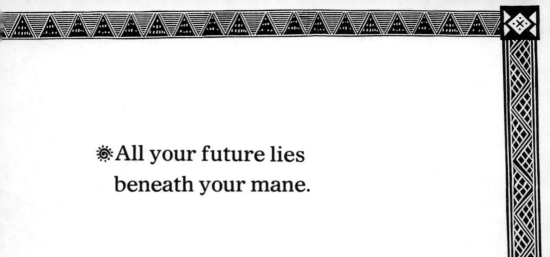

☀ All your future lies
beneath your mane.

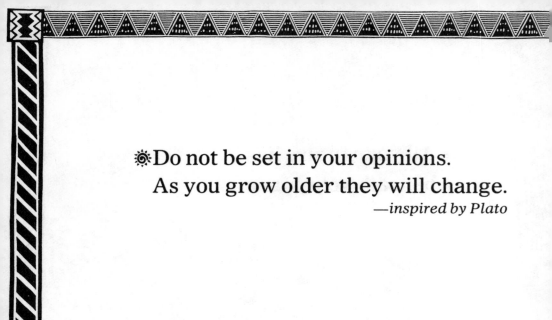

❂Do not be set in your opinions.
As you grow older they will change.
—*inspired by Plato*

☀ A lion king's mind is like a flower—
it flourishes when it is open.

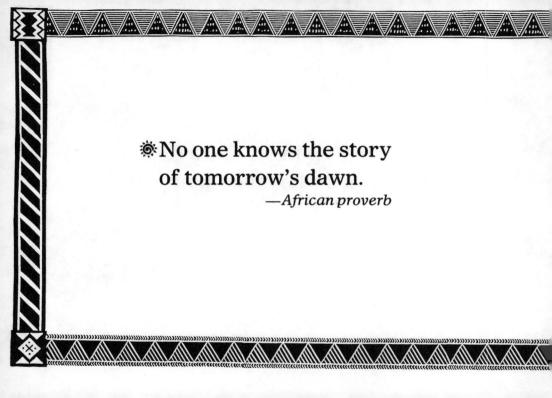

No one knows the story
of tomorrow's dawn.
        —*African proverb*

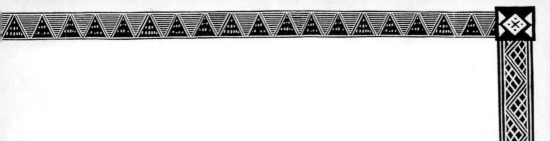

☀ Give advice that you
would take yourself.

❋ The greatest lion king is the
one who still has the
heart of a cub.

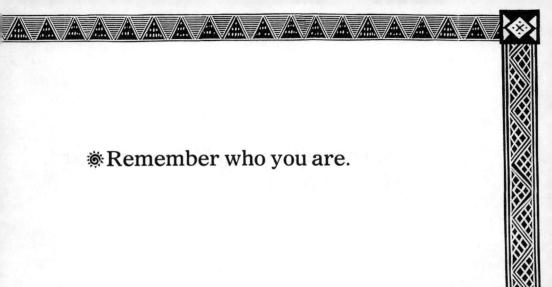

❁ Remember who you are.

☀You can either run from your past
or learn from it.

☀ True friends will be with you
to the very end.

☀ We are all connected
in the great circle of life.

☀ Above all else, *hakuna matata*!